"I am
the Happy
Prince."
"Then why are you
weeping?"
"Because of what I see,"
answered the statue.
"When I was alive, and
had a human heart, I did
not know what tears were —
I was always rich and happy.
My courtiers loved me so much
that when I died, they made
me into a statue. Then they placed me
on this pedestal, high above the city. From
here I can see all the ugliness and misery
of the city. And though my heart now
is made of lead I cannot help but weep."
Three more tears rolled down the

Prince's face. Then he spoke again. "In a little street on the dark side of town, a poor woman spends each day sewing at the window of her house. Her face is thin and tired. Her body is racked with grief. Her little boy lies in bed in the corner. He has a fever, and is crying out for oranges. But his mother is so poor that she can give him nothing but water.

"Please, dear Swallow, help me. Take the ruby from my sword and give it to her."

"But I'm on my way to Egypt," said the swallow. "I must fly on, right away. All my friends are waiting for me, and the snows will soon arrive."

"Just help me for one night," the Prince pleaded, "and be my messenger. The boy is so thirsty — and his mother is so sad."

So the swallow picked out the ruby from the Prince's sword and flew over the rooftops to the little house.

back to the Happy Prince to say goodbye.

"Can you not stay one more night, little Swallow?"

"My friends are waiting for me, and the winter is almost here. How can I stay?"

"On the dark side of the city, there is a young man hunched over a desk. He's trying to write, but the fire has gone out

The poor woman was so tired that she had fallen asleep over her sewing. She did not stir when the bird hopped through the window and laid the ruby down by her thimble. The little boy tossed and turned on his bed, burning with fever. The swallow fanned his hot cheeks with his wings, then flew back to the Prince.

"It's strange," he said, "but although it is so cold I feel much warmer now."

"That's because you have done a kind deed," replied the Prince. And the swallow slept peacefully.

Next day the swallow flew around the town, admiring the sights. When he passed the poor woman's house, he saw that the boy was over his fever, and was standing at the window with a basket full of oranges. "Look Mummy — a swallow, so close to winter." His mother hugged her son and smiled.

As night drew in, and the stars appeared to guide him, the swallow flew

and he's too poor to buy fuel. His fingers are too cold to grip the pen. Pluck out one of my sapphire eyes and take it to him."

"Oh Prince," the swallow gasped, "I cannot do that!" And he began to weep.

"Swallow, Swallow, little Swallow! Do as I command."

So the swallow plucked out the Prince's eye and flew to the writer's house. The poor young man was sitting at his desk, with his head in his hands and heard nothing when the swallow fluttered through a hole in the roof. The little bird placed the jewel on the table, then departed as quietly as he had arrived.

Raising his head from his hands, the young man saw the precious sapphire and gasped with surprise. "What's this! I must have a secret admirer! Oh, now I can buy wood for the fire — and finish my story!"

The next day, the swallow watched the ships in the harbour preparing to set sail. His heart sang for joy. "Tonight I am going to Egypt!" he cried — but nobody heard. And when the moon rose he flew back to the Happy Prince. "I have come to say goodbye!"

it with joy. "What a pretty piece of glass," she said, and ran home laughing.

The swallow felt so warm and happy that he flew back to the Prince and said, "You are blind now. I will stay with you always."

"No, little Swallow," said the poor Prince. "Go away to Egypt."

"I will stay with you always," said the swallow, and slept at the Prince's feet.

All next day he sat on the Prince's shoulder, and told him stories of the strange lands he had seen. The Prince listened and then said, "Fly over my city, little Swallow, and tell me what you see!"

So the swallow flew over the city and saw the rich people in their beautiful houses, eating and dancing and laughing. Then he flew over the drab streets where the poor people lived, and saw the starving children huddled together for warmth.

"Swallow, little Swallow, stay with me just one more night," said the Prince.

"But it's almost winter, and the snows are coming! I *must* fly to Egypt and join my friends — if I don't go now, there will be nowhere left for me to build my nest!"

The Prince was silent for a moment, then he said, "There is a little match-girl down there in the square. She hasn't sold any matches all day, and when she goes home her father will beat her. She has no stockings or shoes, and her little head is bare. Pluck out my other eye and give it to her!"

"I will stay here with you one more night — but I cannot pluck out your eye! You would be blind."

"Swallow, little Swallow, do as I command."

So the bird plucked out the Prince's other eye, and swooped down to the match-girl. He dropped the shimmering sapphire into her palm and she looked at

When he told the Prince what he had seen, the Prince said, "I am covered in fine gold. You must pick it off, leaf by leaf and take it to the poor."

So the swallow picked away the gold, leaf by leaf, until the Happy Prince looked dull and grey. Then he carried it to the poor. As he dropped the gold at the children's feet, the swallow was gladdened to see their faces grow rosier, and hear their happy laughter.

Then the snow fell, soft and heavy on the rooftops. The swallow grew colder and colder and flapped his wings to keep warm. He would not leave the Prince, for he loved him dearly, but he knew he was going to die. He just had the strength to fly up to the Prince's shoulder one last time.

"Are you going south at last, little Swallow? You've stayed far too long. Kiss me before you go, for I love you."

"I cannot fly to Egypt, Prince," said the swallow. "I am going to die." And he kissed the Happy Prince on the lips and fell dead to the ground— a bundle of crumpled feathers in the wind. At that moment, there was a sharp crack. The Prince's leaden heart had broken in two. Early next morning, the mayor and the town councillors were walking by when they paused to look up at the statue.

"Oh dear," said the mayor. "Just look at the Happy Prince. The ruby's gone from his sword, his eyes are missing, and his gold has peeled off. What can have happened? He looks no better than a beggar. And what's this dead bird doing here? Throw it on the rubbish heap and put up a notice: *Birds are forbidden to die here.* It really is too bad!"

They pulled down the statue of the
Happy Prince and melted him down in a
furnace — to make a new statue, of the
mayor.

But the Prince's leaden heart would
not melt in the furnace. "That's strange,"
said the foreman when he found it, and he
tossed it carelessly on the rubbish heap,
beside the dead swallow.

"Bring me the two most precious
things in the city," said God to one of his
angels. And the angel returned with the
leaden heart and the dead bird.

"You have made the right choice,"
said God. "For in my garden of Paradise,
this tiny bird will sing for ever, and the
Happy Prince will live in my city of gold."

The Princess Who Met The North Wind

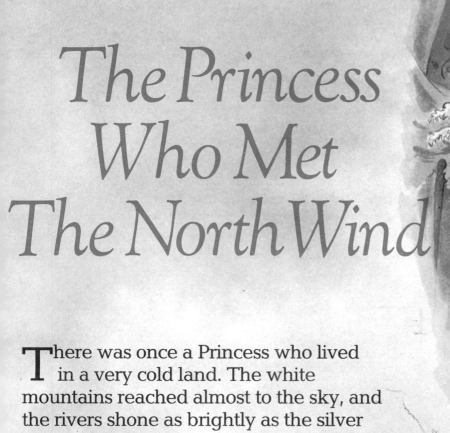

There was once a Princess who lived in a very cold land. The white mountains reached almost to the sky, and the rivers shone as brightly as the silver chain the Princess wore around her neck.

The King and Queen loved their daughter very much and gave her beautiful presents each birthday, but the time came when she had far too much of everything.

"Not another ruby snowbird's egg," said the Princess crossly as she opened up her parcels. "I have three already! And you can take away these pearls — I have so many I could play marbles with them."

"But my child, what *can* we give you?" asked the poor King, wringing his hands. "I've searched high and low to find you something different this year."

"I've told you, father," replied the Princess stamping her foot in annoyance. "I want the most beautiful jewels in the world to hang from the chain around my neck. I'm going to forget about birthdays until you manage to find them for me."

11

So she marched off to bed, taking no notice of her cake which was built in the shape of an iceberg. The King shook his head sadly and gave the pearls to the youngest parlourmaid.

That night, as the Princess lay sleeping, the North Wind began to call and blow around her room at the top of the palace. He blew so fiercely, the heavy clouds rolled away across the sky and the stars shone, clear and bright, into the bedroom. The Princess thought it must be daylight and sat up in bed, staring and blinking.

"Come to the window," sang the North Wind, "and I will give you the most beautiful jewels in the world for the chain around your neck."

The Princess ran to the window and looked up at the sky, where thousands of stars were twinkling and glistening.

"Oh, how beautiful," she whispered. "If only I could reach them."

"Put on your warm cloak and shoes and come with me, Princess," said the North Wind. And he led her down the stairs, through the palace gates, and up the side of the highest mountain in the kingdom.

"I must have the stars for my necklace!" she cried. And she began to slide and slither down the mountain, tearing her cloak and cutting her hands on the rocks.

The Princess did not know that the cold breath of the North Wind had frozen the lake below the mountain, and that all she could see was the reflection of stars from the sky above. She reached the bottom of the mountain, ran to the lake, stretched out her hand for the nearest star and gave a cry of bitter disappointment.

The Princess was not at all happy on the mountain. Her feet were wet, her hands numb, and all the time the North Wind blew, so that her cloak billowed all round her. The more she climbed, the further away the stars seemed to be, twinkling and laughing.

"They are so beautiful," she gasped to the North Wind, "but there must be and easier way to reach them."

"Look down, look down," said the North Wind. And the Princess stared in surprise, for now the stars were below as well as above her, and the whole night seemed on fire with them.

taught you not to be selfish," he said. "I am the Prince of the North Wind, and I have given you the most beautiful jewels in the world."

He took the Princess by the hand and led her back to the palace, where there was much laughter and rejoicing.

The North Wind blew so hard that the pine-trees shivered and the snow fell from their branches on to the Princess. She tried to pull her cloak together, but it was badly torn.

"Oh why did I ever think that I could capture the stars?" she said. "I'm certainly being punished for my silliness, for here I am at the bottom of a mountain, hungry, frozen and miles from home."

As the Princess thought of her warm bed, and the birthday tea she had refused to eat, and the kindness of her mother and father, three tears trickled down her nose and chin and hung, frozen, to her silver necklace.

Suddenly the branches of the pine-trees stopped shivering and all was still. A young man appeared at the side of the Princess, and pointed to the frozen tears which clung to her necklace, gleaming green, purple and blue in the Northern Lights.

"My father, the North Wind, has

Can You Keep A Secret?

In the middle of the big green forest stood a little old house. In it lived a blacksmith and his three pretty daughters. Tansy, the eldest, was dark. Celandine, the second, was fair. Grindelia, the youngest, had hair as brown and glossy as a harvest mouse and eyes as blue as cornflowers. But Tansy and Celandine were forever teasing her because she was so forgetful.

"Watch the pot until we return," her father said as he and her two sisters set off to market. And five minutes later Grindelia was trying to remember what she had been told to do. At last she decided it must have been the spinning.

By the time the others came home, she had spun ten skeins of wool. But, oh dear! The stew was *burnt!*

"You are the most forgetful girl that ever was!" they scolded.

One green and golden day, a Prince came riding through the forest. When he saw the little house, he got off his horse and knocked at the door.

When Tansy opened it, he thought she was the prettiest girl he had ever seen — until he looked over her shoulder and saw Celandine and Grindelia. "I declare, you are each as pretty as the other."

The Prince made up his mind that one of them should be his wife. But how was he to choose between them? "I will marry whichever one of you can keep a secret," he told them. The three hid their faces in their aprons and said, "Oh!"

"Can you keep a secret, Tansy?" the Prince asked.

"I hope so," Tansy answered.

"We'll see." And he whispered in her ear.

"Oh! Fancy that!" said Tansy.

"I will come back in seven days," the Prince told her. "If my secret has been kept, you shall be my wife."

No sooner had he ridden away than Celandine and Grindelia began to ask what the Prince had whispered. But Tansy refused to say. "It's a secret!"

But, as the days went by, Tansy longed to tell the secret to someone else! At last she thought, "I will go and whisper it down the well. That's as good as telling someone, but it will stay a secret." So off she went to the well, and leaning over the edge she whispered the Prince's secret aloud.

"Now I feel much better!"

On the seventh day the Prince came back. "Have you kept my secret, Tansy?"

"Yes indeed, your majesty."

He asked Celandine and Grindelia, "Has she told you my secret?"

"No, she has not," they replied. So the Prince held out his hand to Tansy. "Then, you shall be my w . . ."

But before he could say 'wife', in at the door hopped a little green frog. "Stop!" he croaked. "She told *me*! She came and whispered it into the well. I was at the bottom and I heard it!"

The minute he was out of sight, Tansy and Grindelia asked her what the Prince had whispered. But Celandine would not tell. "It's a secret!"

But — oh dear! — as the seven days went by, the secret was more and more hard to keep. If only she could share it with someone! At last she thought, "I'll go and whisper it in the orchard. That's as good as telling someone, but it will stay a secret." So off she went to the orchard, where the tops of the trees were floating in pink and white blossom. She stood beneath a fruit tree and whispered the Prince's secret out loud.

"Now I feel much better!"

And there and then the frog croaked out the Prince's secret. "There is a hole in the heel of your left sock!" The Prince let go of Tansy's hand and looked at her sadly. "In that case, I'm afraid you cannot be my wife," he said. Turning to Celandine he asked, "Can *you* keep a secret?"

"I think so, your majesty."

"We'll see." And he whispered a new secret in her ear.

"Well, I never did!" cried Celandine. "If you keep my secret for a week, you shall be my wife."

17

The next day the Prince came back. "Have you kept my secret, Celandine?"

"Yes, indeed, your majesty."

The prince asked Tansy and Grindelia if their sister had told them the secret. "No, no," came the reply. So he held out his hands to Celandine. "Then you shall be my w . . .".

But before he could say 'wife', there came a buzzing at the window, and in swarmed a cloud of bumble-bees. "Say no more!" droned the bees. "She told *us!* She came to the orchard and whispered it aloud. And we in the trees heard it!" Then the bees hummed the Prince's secret aloud. "There is a hole in the toe of your right sock!"

The Prince let go of Celandine's hand and looked at her sadly. "In that case, I'm afraid you cannot be my wife."

He turned to Grindelia. "Can *you* keep a secret?"

"I don't know, your majesty."

"Let's see." And he whispered a third secret in her ear.

"Well!" exlaimed Grindelia.

Then off the Prince rode to his castle.

Immediately Tansy and Celandine cried, "Tell us what he said!" But Grindelia shook her head and put her hands over her ears. "I can't!"

Now, you remember how forgetful Grindelia was? Well, as the seven days came and went , she grew sadder and sadder. "If only," she sighed. "If only I could *remember* it!"

18

But although she racked her brain, the Prince's secret had gone in one ear and out of the other.

On the seventh day the Prince came back. "Have you kept my secret?"

"No, I haven't," she replied, because she was a very truthful girl. "I've lost it. I've clean forgotten it."

"Forgotten it!" exclaimed the Prince. "Fancy that! Well I never!"

Then he looked at Grindelia's glossy brown hair and eyes the colour of cornflowers. "She's the one for me!" he thought to himself. "I don't care if she can keep a secret or not!" And he took Grindelia's hands in his. "Will you marry me?"

Grindelia looked at the Prince. He had a kind, gentle face, so she said, "Yes," kissed her father and sisters goodbye, and rode off with the Prince.

"She forgot to take off her apron!" they laughed.

No-one ever found out what the Prince had whispered in Grindelia's ear. She and her Prince lived happily together in the castle on the hill, and although Grindelia never had to spin wool or sweep the floor, or watch the pot, she did sit down with a basket of mending and a darning needle every night — for the Prince was terribly hard on his socks.

The PRINCESS and the PEA

Long ago, a young prince lived in a far-off land. But he was not a very happy prince, because he could not find a real princess to marry.

"Oh, you're much too fussy!" said the queen. "I've introduced you to the most beautiful, the most clever, the most charming princesses from here, there and everywhere, but you're never satisfied."

"I'm very grateful to you, mother," the prince replied, "but a *real* princess is very rare. I'm sure I'll find her one day."

In his heart, he knew that somewhere, sometime he would meet her. He would never stop searching. "I've met many girls who call

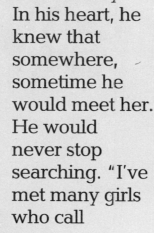

themselves a princess," he said. "The whole world calls them princesses. Some are very beautiful, some are very clever. Many are very charming. But *my* princess will be all these things and more!"

For a year he sailed around the world in search of his perfect bride. He visited palaces in Persia and Peru, castles in China and Spain. But he did not find the face he was looking for. When he returned to his own country, sunny summer was darkening into cold, grey winter.

One night, not long after his return, there was a terrible storm. Thunder roared, lightning flashed, and the icy wind crept in through every window and door in the palace. The prince had gone to bed to keep warm, while the king and queen sat downstairs, reading.

The old king shivered as he pulled his chair closer to the fire. "I'm glad I'm

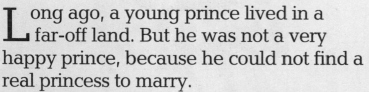

wrapped up here in the warm. I feel very sorry for any of my subjects who are caught in this awful weather."

"Nobody with any sense would be out on such a dreadful night," replied the queen.

Hardly had she spoken when they both heard a knock on the door. And then again, even louder. The king hurried to the hall. He drew back all the bolts and with a great heave pulled the door open. A gust of wind blew freezing sleet into the hall and a flash of lightning lit up the porch.

"Brrrh!" shivered the king. And then, peering into the darkness: "Well, bless my soul! Who are you, my poor girl?"

There, with the storm raging all around her, stood a pretty young girl. Her dress was soaked through, and her shoes were covered in mud. Her long, golden hair hung in damp ringlets round her shoulders.

"I'm a princess," the stranger replied, her teeth chattering.

"Yes, yes, my dear, of course you are," the king smiled. "Well, you had better come in. I must say, though, I've never known a princess to arrive in anything but a grand carriage."

"No, nor have I," thought the queen. "I'll soon find out if she's a real princess or not."

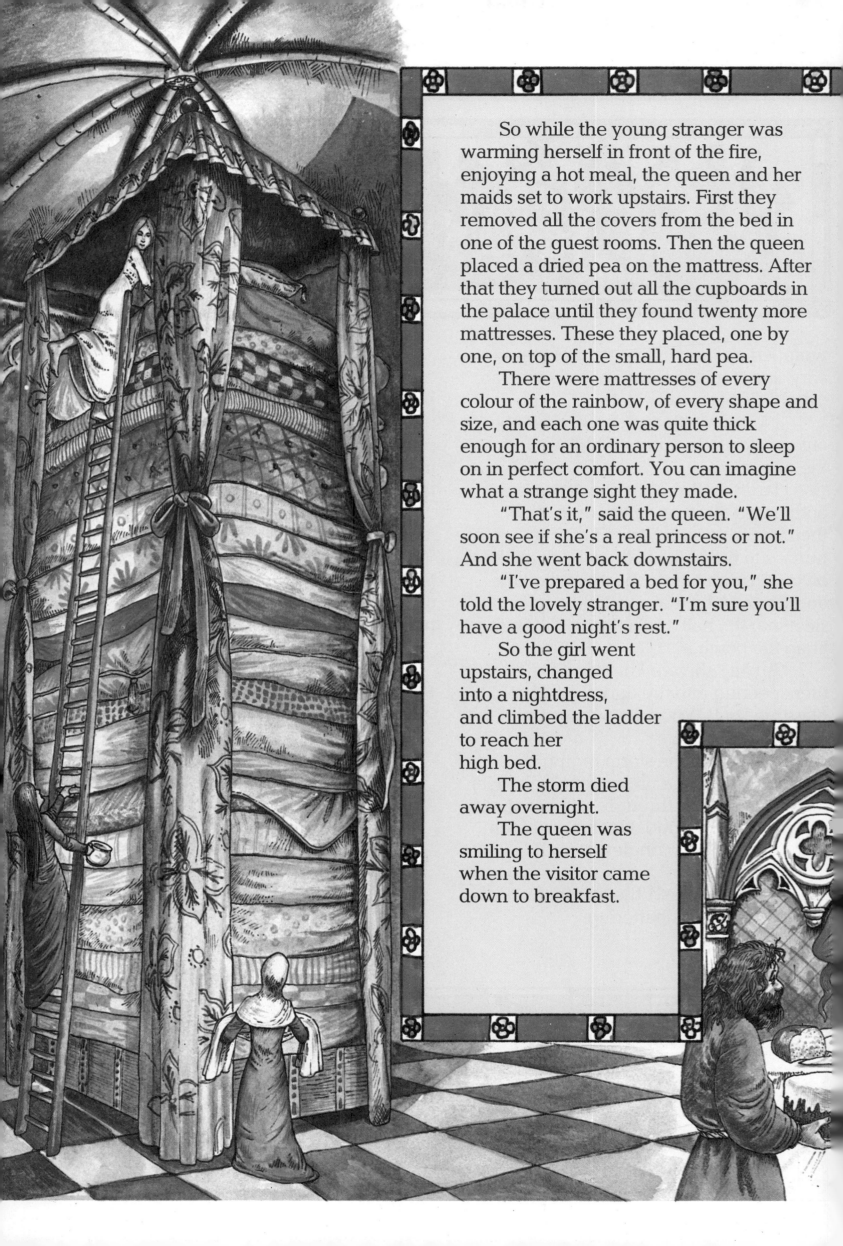

So while the young stranger was warming herself in front of the fire, enjoying a hot meal, the queen and her maids set to work upstairs. First they removed all the covers from the bed in one of the guest rooms. Then the queen placed a dried pea on the mattress. After that they turned out all the cupboards in the palace until they found twenty more mattresses. These they placed, one by one, on top of the small, hard pea.

There were mattresses of every colour of the rainbow, of every shape and size, and each one was quite thick enough for an ordinary person to sleep on in perfect comfort. You can imagine what a strange sight they made.

"That's it," said the queen. "We'll soon see if she's a real princess or not." And she went back downstairs.

"I've prepared a bed for you," she told the lovely stranger. "I'm sure you'll have a good night's rest."

So the girl went upstairs, changed into a nightdress, and climbed the ladder to reach her high bed.

The storm died away overnight.

The queen was smiling to herself when the visitor came down to breakfast.

"And how did you sleep, my dear?" she asked as the girl sat down at the table.

"I'm sorry to say that I didn't sleep well at all," replied the stranger. "It sounds very rude, but even with all those mattresses I was still uncomfortable."

"But that's impossible," said the king. "You had the best bed in the palace!"

The girl blushed, afraid of sounding ungrateful. "Well, I felt as if I was lying on a pebble. And this morning, I'm black and blue all over."

The queen could hardly believe her ears. "Then you are indeed a princess!" she cried. "Only a royal person could have such tender and sensitive skin. Only a real princess could feel a dried pea through twenty-one mattresses!"

That was exactly what the prince thought, too. When he came into the breakfast room, he took one look at the beautiful girl and knew at once *she* was the one he had been dreaming of. He did not need to be introduced. He needed no dried pea, no twenty-one mattresses for proof. His heart told him at once that he had found his true princess.

The king proclaimed a holiday for everyone in the land, so that they could all celebrate the wedding of the prince and princess. And the prince made sure the pea was put on display in a glass case in the city square for all to see.

And do you know . . . to this day it is still there, to remind people of his one and only love, the *real* princess.

Sleeping Beauty

The sun was shining, and the birds were singing, but the queen was sad as she bathed in her lake.

"Oh, how dearly I wish for a child," she sighed, and a tear fell from her eye into the open mouth of a frog who was perched on a water-lily leaf.

"By this time next year you shall have a daughter!" he croaked. Then he dived into the weeds and was gone.

His words came true. The king and queen became the proud, happy parents of a beautiful baby daughter.

"The roses are just beginning to bloom," said the king. "Let's call her Rose, and she shall have the most magnificent christening ever known."

"We must invite all the most important people," said the queen.

"And the thirteen fairies," added the king.

"My love, remember. The law says that fairies must eat from golden plates. We only have twelve golden plates."

"Well, twelve fairies are enough," decided the king.

After the grand feast, the guests danced and sang until it was time for the fairies to present their gifts to the royal baby.

The first gave her Beauty, the second Grace of Movement. The others in turn gave her a Sweet Voice, Kindness, Health, Gentleness, Truth, Goodness, Friendship, Happiness, a Sense of Humour, and . . . But, before the twelfth fairy could speak, the ballroom suddenly turned dark, the wind howled, an owl hooted and everyone shivered.

Standing beside the cradle was a small bent figure dressed all in black. Her green eyes gleamed in a white wrinkled face.

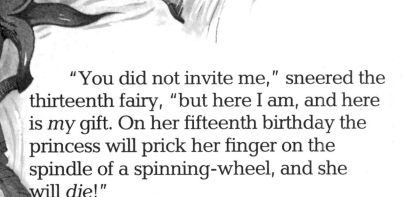

"You did not invite me," sneered the thirteenth fairy, "but here I am, and here is *my* gift. On her fifteenth birthday the princess will prick her finger on the spindle of a spinning-wheel, and she will *die!*"

With these words she vanished. The wind subsided, the owl grew silent, warmth and light returned. In her cradle the tiny princess cried softly and a gloom fell on everyone.

Then the twelfth fairy came forward and spoke quietly: "Rose *will* prick her finger, but she will not die. Instead she and all within the palace will fall asleep, until one day a prince's kiss will wake her."

Immediately the king ordered that every spinning-wheel in the kingdom should be destroyed. Huge bonfires were built in every market square, and a thousand spinning-wheels were burned on them.

The years flew by and Rose grew up happily with the fairies' gifts. She was loved by all who knew her. Then, on her fifteenth birthday, her parents gave her a splendid party.

Shortly before the palace clock struck six, Rose said, "Let's play hide-and-seek." So all the young guests hid in cupboards, under huge tables, and behind heavy curtains. Rose tip-toed up the winding staircase to a turret at the top of a tower where nobody had been for years.

It was very dark and musty and Rose was beginning to wish she had not hidden there when she saw a dusty door. She wrote *Rose* in the dust and then pushed it, gently. It swung slowly open into a tiny room.

"Come in, my dear," whispered a strange voice.

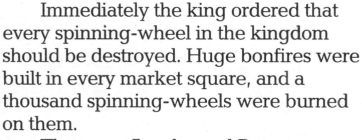

And there in the gloom, Rose saw an old woman, dressed in black, sitting before a large wheel. The room grew darker, the wind blew outside and an owl hooted. Rose shivered.

"What's that?" she asked.

"Why, a spinning-wheel, my dear."

The old woman turned her pale, wrinkled face with its gleaming green eyes towards the Princess. "I'm making the cloth for a sheet. Come closer . . . see how the spindle dances as the thread runs round it."

Rose was fascinated, she had never seen a spinning-wheel before. She held out her hand to touch the bobbing spindle. "It hurts. Oh, it hurts,"

she cried. She had pricked her finger — and immediately she fell into a deep sleep.

Outside, the wind subsided, the owl grew silent, warmth and light returned. The old woman had vanished.

Sitting on their thrones, the king and queen suddenly stopped in the middle of a conversation and fell asleep. The young guests slept in their hiding places, their fingers on lips that were about to say *sh!* and the seeker slept standing up, his hands firmly over his eyes.

The clock stopped ticking. A fly hung poised in mid-air. The cook's cat slept outside a mouse-hole, and the frightened mouse slept inside. The cook fell asleep with her hand raised ready to slap the naughty kitchen boy. The poor boy slept, still unsmacked across her knee, while the goblet he had broken lay in pieces on the floor.

The dog, who had been dozing, slept still more soundly. The spiders were still and silent in their webs in the turret room. Days and then weeks passed. Months turned into years.

After ten years, a hedge of briar roses had grown up all around the palace. After twenty, the palace was hidden completely. Ninety years passed and the thicket of roses, weeds and thistles had grown into a dense forest.

The story of the Sleeping Beauty spread throughout the world, and was passed down in every royal family. Many brave princes tried to break through the forest to find her, but none succeeded . . . until, one day, a handsome prince arrived from a far-off land. Though cruelly scratched by the thorns and brambles he went on hacking his way through the thicket with his sword until he grew exhausted. His strength had almost given out when suddenly something very strange happened. The cruel thorns softened, and roses began to bloom on the briars. He moved as though by magic through the branches.

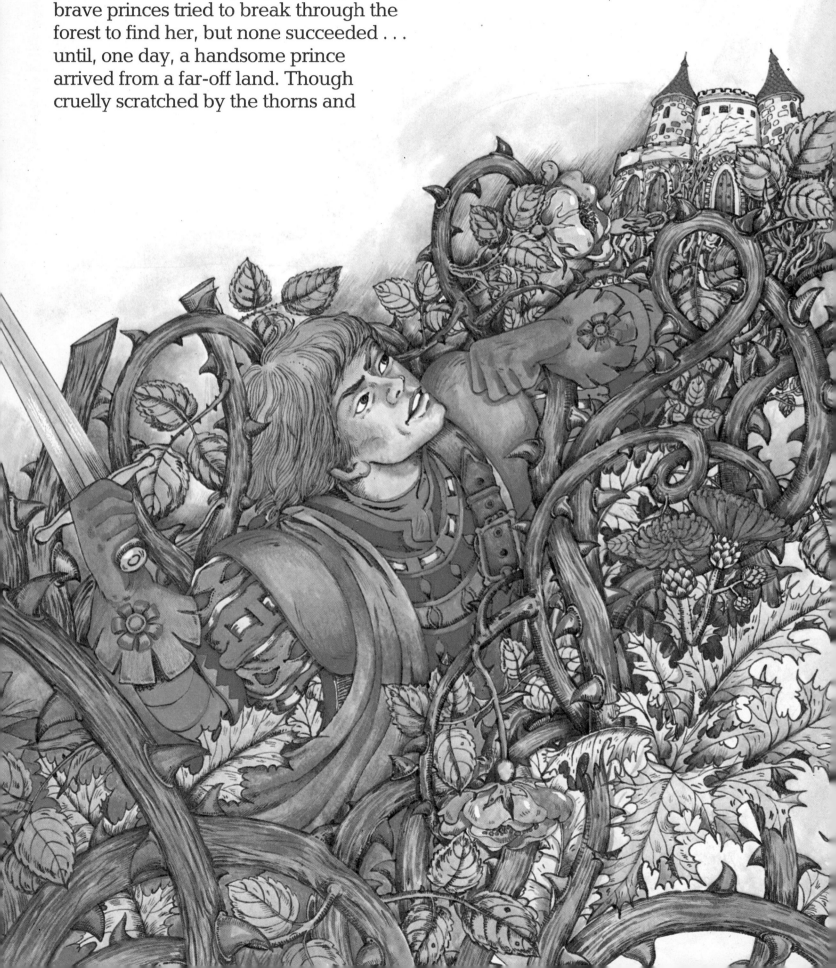

A hundred years had passed since Rose's fifteenth birthday, but in the palace time had stood still. The prince opened the heavy palace doors. He passed among the frozen party-goers and climbed the same winding staircase the princess had climbed a hundred years before.

At the top of the staircase he saw the letters *Rose* on the dusty door. And inside the turret room, he found the sleeping girl. He had never seen anyone so beautiful. Slowly, as if in a dream, he bent his head and kissed her.

The princess woke immediately. "I have waited for you *so* long," she said, gazing up at him."

At once everyone in the palace awoke. The king turned to the queen and said, "I quite agree with you, my dear." The mouse scuttled further down the hole away from the hissing cat. The dog rolled over. The seeker took his hands from his eyes, and called out "Ready!" and the children hiding smiled, fingers on lips and whispered *sh!* The naughty kitchen boy scrambled off the cook's lap and she slapped her own knee instead. The fly landed on a jammy spoon, and the palace clock struck six.

Many years later, when Rose and the prince were married, they would often tell their children the strange tale of the thirteenth fairy, the spindle, and the hundred sleeping years.

THE HAPPY PRINCE

High above the city, on a tall stone column, stood the beautiful statue of the Happy Prince. His body was covered in thin leaves of fine gold, his eyes were two sparkling sapphires, and a large red ruby glowed in his sword-hilt.

"How happy the Prince looks," the townspeople would say, as they wandered through the square. "What a pity we can't all be happy like him."

One night, a swallow flew over the city. Winter was coming, and he was flying south to the warmth and sunshine, charting his course by the stars. All the other swallows had gone weeks before, but this one had lingered behind. Now he was hurrying to join his friends before the snows arrived.

When the swallow saw the golden prince at the top of the stone column, he stopped to take a rest. "What a wonderful statue," he thought. "I'll perch between its feet to keep out of this wind.

"But just as he was folding his wings, a large drop of water splashed down beside him. "Rain? On such a clear, starry night?"

A second drop fell. Then another. The swallow shook his feathers irritably. "What use is a statue if it doesn't keep the rain off!" Then he looked up at the Prince and what did he see? The drops were not rain at all, but tears, trickling slowly down from the Prince's golden cheeks.

"Who are you?" asked the swallow, full of wonder.

4

Tales of Princes and Princesses

CONTENTS

Marshall Cavendish